BILLY BUTTON
≋ *Telegram Boy* ≋

SALLY NICHOLLS

Illustrated by Sheena Dempsey

First published in 2016 in Great Britain by
Barrington Stoke Ltd
18 Walker Street, Edinburgh, EH3 7LP

www.barringtonstoke.co.uk

Text © 2016 Sally Nicholls
Illustrations © 2016 Sheena Dempsey

The moral right of Sally Nicholls and Sheena Dempsey to
be identified as the author and illustrator of this work has
been asserted in accordance with the Copyright, Designs and
Patents Act, 1988

A CIP catalogue record for this book is available
from the British Library upon request

ISBN: 978-1-78112-532-8

Printed in China by Leo

This book is super readable for young readers beginning
their independent reading journey.

To Tara, brightest of the buttons

Contents

CHAPTER 1

The Post Office

Once, there was a village. In the village there was a shop. And above the shop lived Mr Button, Mrs Button and their son Billy.

Mrs Button ran the shop. It sold all sorts of things –

- lollipops and balls of string

- chocolate cake and milk

- newspapers and glue.

Everybody in the village shopped there.

"The nicest thing about running a shop is the people," Mrs Button said. Mrs Button liked people.

At the back of the shop was a window and behind the window was a little room full of parcels and brown paper. This was the post office. It was Mr Button's job to run the post office.

"From our village," Mr Button said, "you can send a letter to anywhere in the world. To Africa! To America! To Australia!"

Mr Button was very proud of his post office.

"The Royal Mail," he said. He shook his head. "What a wonderful thing!"

CHAPTER 2

Red Bike Boy

In those days, there were no computers. There were no text messages, no emails and no internet. If you wanted to send someone an urgent message, you had to send a telegram.

A telegram was a bit like an old-fashioned text message. If you wanted to send a telegram to your granny, you

could ring up Mr Button at the post
office and tell him your message. Or you
could come to the post office and write it
down on a special notepad. The writing
in the notepad had to be all in CAPITAL
letters like this –

GRANNY SMITH 4 CHURCH LANE
MANCHESTER STOP HAPPY BIRTHDAY
GRANNY STOP LOVE ANNA

You had to put your granny's name and address as part of the telegram. And you had to write "STOP" a lot to show where the full stops went in your telegram.

Then Mr Button would ring up the post office in Manchester and someone in Manchester would write down your message and put it in a small brown envelope. Then they would give the envelope to a telegram boy.

Telegram boys were very smart. They wore blue uniforms with blue hats and shiny Royal Mail badges. They rode about on red bicycles. A telegram boy would ride his bicycle as fast as he could to your granny's house and give her your message in its brown envelope.

There was a telegram boy who worked for Mr Button. His name was Charlie.

"When I grow up," Billy Button said, "I'm going to be a telegram boy and ride a red bicycle just like Charlie."

CHAPTER 3

A Job for Billy

One sunny day at the start of the summer holidays, Mr Button came into the post office. He looked very serious. "Have you heard the news?" he said to Mrs Button.

"What news?" said Mrs Button.

"Charlie fell out of a tree," said Mr Button. "He's broken his leg. He won't be able to ride a bicycle for weeks and weeks."

"Oh no!" said Mrs Button. "Poor Charlie. But what are you going to do?"

"I don't know," said Mr Button. "It's a worry. All the boys in the village have jobs already."

Billy was pretending to stack the tins – but he was listening really – and he had a great idea.

"I could be a telegram boy," he said. "I could! And it's the summer holidays, so I don't have to go to school. And I could ride Charlie's red bicycle. Oh, let me! Please!"

Mr and Mrs Button looked at each other.

"I don't know ..." Mr Button said. "The Post Office Rules say telegram boys have to be 14. They're very clear."

"But Billy is a very grown-up sort of boy and the Post Office would never know," Mrs Button said. "Not if we didn't tell them. I think it's a good idea."

"So do I!" said Billy. "You could pay me. I could save up and buy my own bicycle."

"All right, all right," said Mr Button. "You'd better come with me."

Mr Button took Billy to the store cupboard. He pulled out a leather belt and a leather pouch and gave them to Billy.

"You wear the pouch on your belt," he said. "And make sure you polish the buckle so that it's always nice and shiny."

Billy opened the pouch. Inside was a telegram notebook, a pencil, six pennies and a copy of the Post Office Rules.

"You need to have a read of that,"
Mr Button said. "All telegram boys must
obey the Post Office Rules." He looked
at the rules himself. "Oh dear," he said.
"You're a bit short. And a bit skinny.
Are you 25 inches around the chest?"

"I don't know," Billy said. "You could
measure me."

"Let's not worry about that now,"
said Mr Button. "The most important

rule is that you must always be polite and smart. And you must never read the telegrams."

"But you always read the telegrams," said Billy.

"That's different," Mr Button said. "I'm the postmaster."

"Oh," said Billy. "So when do I get my uniform?"

"Not just yet," said Mr Button. "You're too small. But you can have a hat and an armband."

The armband was grey, with a red Post Office crown on it. Billy put it on over his jacket sleeve. He felt very proud of how smart it looked.

"There!" Mr Button said. "Now you can get to work."

CHAPTER 4

Three Telegrams

Billy soon found out that a telegram boy's job was very interesting.

First, he had to deliver a telegram to Mr and Mrs Owen.

The telegram said that Mr and Mrs Owen's daughter had had a baby boy called Albert. Mrs Owen was very pleased. She gave Billy a big hug and a slice of plum cake to celebrate.

Then he had to deliver a telegram to the grand house on the hill. This one was for a young lady called Lucy, from a young gentleman called John. It said that John was going to come and visit at the weekend.

Lucy was very pleased too. She gave Billy a kiss on the cheek and a rose from the garden. Billy would have rather had some more cake. But he remembered the Post Office Rules and said, "Thank you very much."

Then Billy had to deliver a telegram to the vicar. It said that the vicar's sister was ill in hospital, and could the vicar come and visit? The vicar was so worried about his sister that he didn't give Billy anything. Not even a "thank you". But Billy didn't mind.

He knew that a telegram boy's job was very important. It wasn't just about roses and plum cake.

CHAPTER 5

A Telegram for Mr Grundle

The next day, a telegram arrived at the post office for Mr Grundle.

"That's funny," Mr Button said. "Mr Grundle's never had a telegram before."

"Who's it from?" said Mrs Button.

"Someone called Alice," Mr Button said. He read the telegram out loud.

IN ENGLAND STOP CAN I COME STAY ON TUESDAY STOP ALICE

"Ooh!" said Mrs Button. "Mr Grundle's never had a visitor before either. I wonder who Alice is. Maybe she's a lady friend?"

Billy giggled. "I wouldn't want to be Mr Grundle's lady friend!" he said.

Mr Grundle was old and very grumpy. He lived by himself in a tumbledown cottage on the edge of the village. One autumn, Billy and two of his friends stole some apples from the tree in his garden. Mr Grundle was so angry he threw his boot at Billy. And then he went to the post office to complain.

"You ought to beat that boy!" he told Mr Button.

That made Mr Button very angry. "I don't beat my son," he said.

When Mr Grundle had gone, Mr Button said to Billy, "I wish you'd stolen his boot, too!"

But now what Mr Button said to Billy was, "The reply's been paid. That means Mr Grundle can answer the telegram and he doesn't have to pay. He can have 15 free words. Off you go. And don't be cheeky."

Billy rode very slowly to Mr Grundle's cottage. When Mr Grundle came to the door, Billy said, "Telegram," and gave Mr Grundle the small brown envelope.

Mr Grundle opened the envelope and read the telegram. Then a funny thing happened. His cheeks went pink. His mouth twitched and he almost looked like he was smiling.

"Any reply?" Billy said. "It's paid for."

"Yes," said Mr Grundle.

Billy took out his pad and gave it to Mr Grundle, but Mr Grundle shook his head.

"My old hands are too sore to write," he said. "You write it. Put this –"

ALICE HOPE 4 IVY LANE NEWCASTLE
STOP CAN'T WAIT STOP WILL MAKE
BUNS STOP GEORGE

'Buns?' Billy thought. But he didn't
say anything. He put the pad back in his
pouch and cycled away.

CHAPTER 6

Nosy Parkers

"Buns?" said Mr Button, when he read Mr Grundle's telegram.

"Buns?" said Mrs Button.

But buns it was.

The next day, Mr Grundle came into Mrs Button's village shop. He bought flour, sugar, butter, eggs and a whole bag of currants.

"Buns," said Mrs Button, when he'd gone. "Currant buns, no less."

On Monday afternoon, Mr Grundle came into the post office to use the public telephone.

"I want to order a taxi for tomorrow morning," he said. "I need to go to the barber's in town."

As he put down the phone, Mr Button smiled at him. "Getting a haircut?" he said.

Mr Grundle frowned. He muttered something about nosy parkers and stamped out of the shop.

Early on Tuesday morning, Mr Grundle got into a taxi and drove into town.

When he'd gone, a new telegram arrived at the post office. It said –

BUS GETS IN 11 A.M. STOP CAN YOU MEET ME STOP ALICE

"Oh no!" said Mrs Button. "Mr Grundle's gone to town. He won't be back in time! Alice won't know what to do."

"Billy," said Mr Button. "This is a Royal Mail emergency. You must go and meet Alice from the bus. Bring her back to the shop for a cup of tea."

CHAPTER 7

Rucksacks and Walking Sticks

Three people got off the bus. One was Mr Johnson the butcher. One was Susan Johnson, his little girl. And one was Alice.

Alice was tall and very brown, with white hair and bright green eyes. She

was wearing a green hat and carrying a
walking stick and a rucksack.

Billy went up to her.

"Good morning," he said. "I'm afraid Mr Grundle has gone to town, so I couldn't give him your telegram. Would you like to wait in our shop until he comes back? We could make you a cup of tea."

Alice looked at Billy, and her whole face smiled.

"A cup of tea," she said, "would be lovely."

Mrs Button made Alice a cup of tea, and Mr Button gave her the best post office chair to sit on. Billy took her rucksack and her walking stick and put them in the back of the shop.

"Oooh," Alice said. "This tea is wonderful. Thank you. Do you know," she said to Billy, "I've been in Africa for 30 years. Africa's a grand place. But I did miss English tea."

"What were you doing in Africa?" Billy said. He wasn't interested in tea, English or otherwise, but he was interested in Africa.

"I was a teacher in a little school in Kenya," said Alice. She sighed. "I loved it. I used to sit in my garden in the evenings and watch the elephants walking past. But then I got too old to teach any more. So I came home."

"And how do you know Mr Grundle?" said Mrs Button. She looked so curious that Billy wanted to laugh.

Alice sighed again. "He used to live next door to me," she said. "We were the best of friends. He wanted to marry me, but I wanted to have adventures and travel the world. I haven't seen him in 30 years!"

"And what are you going to do now you're back in England?" Mr Button asked.

Alice took a sip of her tea and looked up from her cup.

"I don't know," she said, and her green eyes shone. "But I'm looking forward to finding out!"

When they saw Mr Grundle's taxi come down the road, Billy ran out of the shop and waved. Mr Grundle came into the shop. He seemed rather cross to see Alice there.

"Oh, don't frown," Alice said. "They've been so kind to me. What a lovely village you live in."

"Humph," said Mr Grundle.

CHAPTER 8

Alice and Mr Grundle

Alice stayed with Mr Grundle for a whole week.

They went fishing.

They did the gardening.

They ate currant buns in the garden.

On Sunday, they went to church.
Alice sang all the songs in a loud, clear
voice. Mr Grundle looked a bit surprised.
Then he really did smile. Then he joined
in.

Billy joined in too. He liked singing.

After church, Alice came to say "hello" to Mr and Mrs Button and Billy.

"We made you some currant buns," she said. "To say thank you for looking after me."

They stood together outside the church and ate the buns.

"These buns taste wonderful," Mrs Button said. "Are you having a good holiday?"

Alice beamed.

"Oh, I am!" she said. "I'm so happy, I could stay here for ever."

But on Monday afternoon, Billy looked out of the post office window and saw Alice sitting on her rucksack at the bus stop. She was crying.

"Oh my goodness!" Mrs Button said, as she peered out of the window. "That poor woman! Go and see what's the matter at once."

Billy went and sat on the grass beside Alice. "What's the matter?" he said.

Alice wiped her face with her hankie.

"Oh dear," she said. "I feel so bad. George – that's Mr Grundle – asked me to marry him and I said no. And now he's so cross!"

"Why did you say no?" Billy said. "Don't you like him?"

"Of course I like him," said Alice. "But ... well. I don't have much money. I don't mind. I don't need money. But if I married George, people would say it was because I had nowhere else to live. They'd say I was using him. They'd say I couldn't look after myself."

"They could say that," Billy said, "but it's not true."

"No," said Alice. "Of course it isn't true."

"So what does it matter?" Billy said.

"I don't know," said Alice. She sniffed. "But it matters to me."

The bus pulled up at the bus stop. Alice picked up her rucksack.

"Don't go!" said Billy.

But Alice got onto the bus.

"Goodbye," she said. "Tell your mother and father I'll miss them."

And the bus drove away and Alice was gone.

CHAPTER 9

Another Telegram for Mr Grundle

Mr and Mrs Button both looked very serious when Billy told them what Alice had said.

"Poor Alice!" said Mrs Button.

"Poor Mr Grundle!" said Mr Button.

"Maybe she'll change her mind," said Billy.

"Maybe," said Mr Button. But he didn't sound very hopeful.

For a whole week, Mr Grundle stamped around the village in a bad mood. He shouted at Mrs Button because the shop had run out of his favourite biscuits. He shouted at Billy and his friends for kicking a football up and down the street.

"It's because he misses Alice," Billy said. "That's why."

But on Tuesday, a new telegram came into the post office. Mr Button got very excited when he read it.

"Listen to this!" he said, and he waved the telegram in the air.

I'M SORRY I WAS STUPID STOP PLEASE

FORGIVE ME STOP WOULD LOVE TO

MARRY YOU STOP ALICE

"Hurrah!" Mrs Button cried.

"Quick!" said Mr Button. "There's no time to lose." He stuffed the telegram in an envelope and gave it to Billy. "Off you go," he said. "The reply's paid."

Billy rode as fast as he could to Mr Grundle's house and banged on the door.

"Telegram!" he called.

Mr Grundle opened the door. He looked grumpier than ever.

"Who's it from?" he said.

Billy hesitated.

"Come on," Mr Grundle said. "I know your father reads all my telegrams."

"It's from Alice," said Billy.

Mr Grundle began to close the door.

"Don't!" Billy cried. "Don't you want to know what she said?"

"I don't care what she said," Mr Grundle shouted. "Go away!"

"Don't you want to reply?" said Billy. "The reply's paid."

Mr Grundle didn't answer. He slammed the door and Billy heard his footsteps stomping back into his house.

Billy knocked and knocked on the door. But Mr Grundle didn't answer.

Billy sat on the step and wondered
what to do.

Then he had an idea.

It was a risky idea.

It wasn't very honest.

And it was definitely against the Post Office Rules.

But it just might work.

He opened his pouch and took out the telegram pad. Alice had paid for a 15-word reply.

In his best writing, Billy wrote –

ALICE HOPE 4 IVY LANE NEWCASTLE
STOP YES PLEASE COME AT ONCE
STOP GEORGE

Then Billy put the pad back into his pouch and rode back to the post office as fast as he could.

CHAPTER 10

What Happened Next

The next day, Billy went to deliver another telegram to Lucy, the young lady in the grand house on the hill.

When he came back, Mr and Mrs Button were full of excitement.

"Guess who came on the last bus?" Mrs Button said. "Alice!"

"She went straight to Mr Grundle's house," said Mr Button. "He must be as happy as a songbird."

'Oh dear,' Billy thought. He rushed outside and got straight onto his bicycle and rode to Mr Grundle's house.

Alice was standing on the step, banging on the door.

"Go away!" Mr Grundle shouted from inside.

"But you told me to come," Alice shouted.

Mr Grundle opened the door a tiny crack.

"I did what?" he said.

"You sent me a telegram," said Alice.

"I sent you a telegram?" Mr Grundle said.

They both looked at Billy.

"Um," Billy said. "Mr Grundle didn't read your telegram. So he didn't know you wanted to marry him. Um. So I thought you should come and tell him yourself. Um. Sorry."

"You want to marry me?" Mr Grundle said, looking at Alice.

"Of course I want to marry you," said Alice. "If you'll still have me."

Mr Grundle went bright pink. "Of course I'll still have you," he said. He smiled, and his whole face changed. He looked like quite a different person.

CHAPTER 11

Lots and Lots of Telegrams

Mr Grundle and Alice were married in the village church. Lots of people came. Afterwards, there was food and dancing and lots and lots of cake.

Before the wedding, Alice said to Billy, "You should be Mr Grundle's best man."

But Billy said, "I can't – I'm sorry. I've got work to do."

And so he had. Billy was kept very busy riding from the post office to the church hall, delivering telegrams.

ALICE GRUNDLE ST PETER'S CHURCH
LITTLE HADLEY ENGLAND STOP MUCH
LOVE FROM ALL THE CHILDREN IN
CLASS FIVE KENYA

GEORGE GRUNDLE THE CHURCH
LITTLE HADLEY STOP WELL DONE
STOP LOVE YOUR BIG BROTHER JAMES

WISH WE COULD BE THERE STOP HAVE

A LOVELY DAY STOP MR AND MRS

BUTTON

Even the vicar's sister sent a
telegram. She was much better now and
was very pleased about the wedding.

GEORGE AND ALICE ST PETER'S LITTLE
HADLEY STOP CONGRATULATIONS
STOP BETTY ABBOTT

Billy delivered all the telegrams to
the village hall. Mr Grundle read them
out at the wedding tea and everybody
cheered.

At the end of the day, a very happy Mr Grundle called Billy over and gave him a shilling.

"Telegram boys aren't allowed to take money," Billy said. "It's against the Post Office Rules."

"Oh," Mr Grundle said, and he tucked the shilling into Billy's pouch. "Well. Some rules are there to be broken."

Our books are tested
for children and young people by
children and young people.

Thanks to everyone who consulted on
a manuscript for their time and effort in
helping us to make our books better
for our readers.